GW00992166

Space Academy

Martin Block

2018

INTRODUCTION

When Jayden first arrives at the Space Academy, he is understandably excited. He's the first Terran to ever attend the prestigious school, so he's making history with everything he does.

A couple weeks after he arrives at the Academy, however, things suddenly turn sour. The daughter of a powerful alien warlord has been kidnapped, and all the evidence points to Jayden as her abductor.

Forced to go on the run, Jayden allies with a mysterious figure who is not what he appears.

Part One: Arrival

"And now, if you look out the port window, you should soon be able to see the famous Galactic Academy!"

Following the pilot's instructions, I watched as the large, silver space station slowly came into view. A gigantic structure made from the sturdiest elements in the galaxy, the Galactic Academy was simultaneously solid and awe-inspiring.

Entranced by the view, I softly pinched myself, wondering if this was all just a dream. What was I—a young Terran boy with absolutely no space experience—doing going to the esteemed Galactic Academy?

The answer to that question originated from an event nearly 100 years ago, when in 1969, the American Astronaut Neil Armstrong set foot on the surface of the moon. An extraordinary event at the time, it had repercussions far beyond what anyone could ever have anticipated.

In 2051—just after the colonization of Mars—an alien spacecraft appeared in the skies above the planet Earth. The nations of the world prepared for war, but then, in a surprising move, the aliens held a meeting with the leaders of all nations. Several hours later, a peace treaty between humanity and the aliens—a species called the Zandu—had been signed, and the world would never be the same.

Thanks to technology given us by the Zandu, humanity blossomed, and in 2062, we were invited to join the Galactic Council, a diplomatic organization that spanned the Milky Way. This was an honor, but even better were the perks that came with membership in this famous institution. These included usage of galactic trade routes, access to the galactic knowledge centers and the ability to send promising young cadets to the esteemed Galactic Academy.

Of course, humanity couldn't let just any child be the first human at this prestigious school; it had to be someone special, someone, symbolic. After close to a year of discussion, they finally decided that the great-great-grandson of Neil Armstrong would be an excellent candidate, as it was the moon landing that first put us on the Zandu's radar.

Searching through the famous astronaut's descendants for a child the correct age to enter the Academy, the leaders of humanity finally settled on me, Jayden Armstrong. I was 14 years old at the time, and I was going to be heading to high school the next year.

Before the call that changed everything, my life was relatively dull. I had few good friends, so I spent most of my time either studying or playing holo-games. As a result, when I was given the opportunity to transfer to the Galactic Academy, I jumped at the chance.

I was given a couple of days to say goodbye to everyone before making the trip to the newly-constructed Andrew Williams Spaceport (which is named after the American President who helped write the peace treaty with the Zandu). From there, I boarded the spacecraft that was to take me to my new home.

Now, nearly a week later, the journey is finally coming to a close. My spacecraft is landing in the main hangar bay of the gigantic space station, and soon I'll be the first human being to set foot in the halls of this esteemed establishment.

"Welcome to the Galactic Academy, Jayden Armstrong," the pilot called out over the intercom as the door slid open. "Go show those aliens what humanity's made of!"

Grabbing the single bag of supplies that I'd been allowed to bring, I walked down the ramp. I was expecting to feel triumph at my achievement, but instead, I only felt nervousness. The pilot was right—my actions here would determine the galaxy's opinion of the entire human race.

Suddenly stricken with terror, I was about to turn around and reenter the shuttle when a voice suddenly called out, "Jayden Armstrong, is that you?"

Nervously turning in the direction of the voice, my jaw dropped in shock. The person that had just addressed me was a beautiful teenage human girl!

"Uh…uh…uh…" I stammered, trying to wrap my head around this discovery. I thought I was going to be the first human here. "I…I'm Jayden," I finally managed.

"I'm Alyssa Shak'zar," the girl replied, pointing to the name tag on her shirt. "Principal Jandork asked me to show you around."

"Shak'zar," I rolled the name on my tongue, "Is that Mongolian?"
"Mongolian?" Alyssa asked in confusion, "I don't remember that planet…"

"No, Mongolia is a country back on the Earth," I explained.

"Why would I have a Mongolian name?" the girl stated in reply. "I'm a Zandu."

"Hey, little sister," a new voice broke in, "Who're you talking to?" Turning, I saw a tall male alien with purplish skin and spiky black hair striding toward us.

"This is Jayden Armstrong, the Terran I was telling you about," Alyssa replied, gesturing in my direction. Giggling, she continued, "He thought I was a Terran! Isn't that hilarious!"

The newcomer laughed with his sister, but in his eyes, there was a dark look. "Greetings, Jayden," he finally said, extending a hand. "I'm Tykvas Shak'zar, Alyssa's older brother."

I took the proffered limb as Alyssa said, "I'm sure the two of you would love to get better acquainted, but we really should get going. You know what Jandork's like if his wishes aren't immediately obeyed."

Nodding, Tykvas replied, "Well then, don't let me stop you." Thanking him, Alyssa turned and walked away as I followed closely. I didn't know what it was, but something about the girl's brother just freaked me out, and I was glad to leave him behind.

Show and Tell

For the next hour, I followed Alyssa through the massive space station. She pointed out all the Academy's major attractions, such as the main classrooms, the cafeteria, the athletic center and the holo-gaming room.

Wherever we went, I could feel people staring at me. At first, I was worried that I'd grown a second head or something, but then I realized that in a school with aliens, two heads were probably the norm.

"You're the first Terran they've ever seen," Alyssa whispered, noticing my nervousness. "It's just like this whenever the first member of a new race joins the Academy. Don't worry; it'll wear off quickly."

Turning a corner into the main corridor, we discovered a hulking student terrorizing a pair of smaller ones. "Listen, you little Bangor twerps," the bully—an eight-foot-tall, red-skinned creature that I recognized as belonging to the Brutoss species—growled, "I want to know who put you up to this."

The victims in this act—a pair of diminutive aliens with fluffy green fur—were too shell-shocked to reply, so Alyssa broke in, "Butarus, what's going on here?"

"Someone told Beka and Jonk to stop paying me their lunch credits!" the Brutoss bully replied angrily, motioning to the pair of cowering Bangori. "When I figure out who it is, I'm gonna…"

"It was I," a deep voice interjected from behind us. Spinning around, I saw a tall, thin alien striding down the hallway in our direction. Recognizing him as a Schaddo by his short black fur, spiky head-spines, and sharp face, I cautiously took a step back. The Schaddo were famous for their skills at assassination, so I did not want to get on this one's bad side.

"Nazo," the Brutoss growled, baring his thick teeth, "I should have known you were behind this."

"You need to stop bullying them," the tall Schaddo replied, shaking his head sadly, "Or else I'll need to make you."

That got Butarus's attention. "No! You can't!" the hulking alien replied, taking a step back. "It's against the rules! There's no fighting in the hallways!"

"Who said I'd be fighting you?" Nazo asked, a quizzical look on his face. "There are plenty of ways I can make you stop bullying the Bangori that don't involve physical violence. You should be aware of that, after all."

Suddenly, a horrified look sprouted on the face of the Brutoss. "You don't mean…that was you?" Nazo said nothing, but I noticed that a small smile tugged at the edge of his mouth. "Okay, then," Butarus stated, backing off, "I'll go. But you're going to regret crossing me!"

7

I watched as the hulking alien stalked away, a slight frown on my face. "I'd been hoping," I told Alyssa, "That by going to a space school I'd leave all this bullying behind."

The Zandu girl laughed at my ignorance, but I detected a tinge of sorrow in her voice as she replied, "If you thought that, then you hadn't spent much time in the galaxy. Bullying—like death and taxes—is universal."

I nodded sadly as I watched the Brutoss thug walk away. Along the side of the corridor, I saw the Schaddo bending down to see if the Bangori were all right. "Well," I whispered to Alyssa, "At least the Bangori have a protector."

"Ah, Nazo," the girl replied, nodding. "He's an interesting one. His mother is an important Schaddo politician in the peace movement. However, from the things I've heard, Nazo doesn't share his mother's opinions."

"Then why is he helping the Bangori?"

"The Bangori and the Schaddo share a star system," Alyssa explained, "And they have an alliance dating back thousands of years. The Schaddo may be sneaky, no-good assassins, but they always honor their word. They're funny like that."

With that, we resumed our tour. Alyssa showed me the way to the observatory and engineering bay, as well as how to find an escape pod in the case of a disaster. Finally, she showed me to my quarters, where she bid me farewell.

"It's good to see a Terran here," she told me as she began to leave. "Ever since my father first landed on your planet, my family has had high hopes for your kind."
"Well, I hope I don't disappoint you all," I told her.

"I'm sure you won't," she replied, walking away.

Watching her go, the thought ran through my mind once again that she looked a lot like a Terran. Still, the only Zandu I'd ever seen were males, so who knows? Could the females look like Terrans…right?

Schooling

When I first arrived at the Academy, I'd been worried that I wouldn't make any friends. To my surprise, however, I discovered that I had a lot in common with many of the students on campus. Soon, I'd become friends with nearly half of the other kids, and I was on good terms with most of the rest. (This didn't include Butarus, of course, who appeared to have a general hatred for everyone.)

My best friends, however, were Alyssa, Beka and Jonk (the Bangori I'd seen on my first day), Kaiold (a young Paranoy) and Gafin (a Finan). We did nearly everything together and had a great time.

The classes at the Galactic Academy were also a lot different from what I was used to backing on Earth. Instead of basic science like Chemistry or Biology, we studied the impact of solar flares on the plant life in the Bango system or the effect of placing Syrellian Gel (a Paranoy creation) on the skin of a Lampas Worm.

For math, instead of taking courses like Algebra we studied the amount of time it'd take for a D-Class Frigate to travel from the Alpha Centauri System to the Zandu System (taking wormholes into effect, of course).

History was especially interesting, as it covered major events from across the galaxy, instead of repeating what I already knew about the history of the Earth.

The best class, however, was physical education. Back on Earth, this usually consisted of climbing ropes in a gym or doing push-ups. At the Galactic Academy, however, they took a much different approach.

The Academy's gymnasium is a highly complex hard-light projection room. Every day, a random program is loaded into the room's computer matrix, and the room adapts to give us that experience. On some days, we're hiking through humid jungles with 10-pound backpacks, on others we're scaling icy cliffs, and there were a couple of times where we participated in ancient battles.

The first time I was plopped into the middle of a battle, I was positive that I was going to die. The room was designed to prevent that. However, I did get quite a shock the first time I found an enemy sword stuck in my chest.

Thanks to these...unique...courses and teaching methods and the many friends I'd gathered, the next couple weeks were a blast. I'd never had so much fun in my life, and I hoped that these times would never end.

Unbeknownst to me, however, things were soon going to take a turn for the worse.

Accused

The trouble began on a day three weeks after I joined the Academy. Alyssa hadn't shown up for the class that morning, but according to the teacher, the Zandu girl had the family business that she needed to attend. Content with that explanation, I didn't give it another thought.

Several hours later, however, I was in the cafeteria eating lunch when suddenly, Alyssa's older brother Tykvas came stomping in. Despite my friendship with his sister, Tykvas had always been somewhat cold to me, but now he looked furious.

"Where's my sister?" he demanded, grabbing me by the collar and hefting me into the air.

Stunned by the Zandu's sudden aggression, it took a moment for my brain to come together enough to say, "What? I thought she was with you!"

"Why would she be with me, Terran?" Tykvas asked with a snarl. "I spend my time with older kids; she spends her time with…you…and your friends."

"But this morning, our teacher got a message saying that Alyssa had family business to attend to," I told him, still trying to process this. "I just assumed that she'd be with you…"

"Then how do you explain this?" the Zandu asked,

handing me a slip of paper.

Glancing over the text quickly, my eyes nearly popped out of my head. No…that couldn't be right… Sure that I'd made a mistake, I read the message out loud, "Warlord Garamak Shak'zar, I have your daughter. Leave the Earth alone, or you'll never see Alyssa again. Don't try to contact me…I'll know when you've done what I've asked."

At the table beside where I was standing, Kaiold (my Paranoy friend) said, "Wait, Jayden, you know about the Sub-Solar Installation?"

"What?" I asked, still stunned. "I…No! I don't know anything about this! I didn't write this note—I have no idea what it's talking about!"

"Whatever you say," Kaiold said with a knowing nod. "But in case you're telling the truth, I'll enlighten you. Back when the Zandu first discovered the Earth, they were unsure whether or not you were a threat, so they…"

"Be quiet, Paranoy," Tykvas broke in, holding up a hand to shush my friend. "That's classified information you're talking about."

Kaiold smiled deprecatingly. "I'm a Paranoy," he told the Zandu. "Dealing in classified information is what we do." He paused for a moment to think, then added, "Well, we also do conspiracy theories, but…"

Suddenly, the door to the cafeteria was knocked open, and a trio of armed guards stormed in. Scanning the room, their gazes locked on me. "Um, what's going on?" I asked nervously.

"I called the authorities on you," Tykvas said with a sneer. "They're going to take you in and torture you until you reveal my sister's location!"

"But I didn't do it!" I protested as the guards began walking across the cafeteria in the direction of our table.

"Tell it to the—Ouch!" Tykvas cried out as Kaiold kicked him in the back of the knee. Collapsing to the ground in anguish, the Zandu released my shirt.
"Go!" the Paranoy told me. "I'll hold them off!"

"What?" I asked in confusion.

"If they take you, they'll torture a confession out of you before executing you publicly," Kaiold said. "Your only chance is to find Alyssa before something worse happens!"

I started to respond but paused. He was right—the only way to prove my innocence would be to find Alyssa and get her testimony. Nodding my thanks to the Paranoy, I turned and ran for the cafeteria's back door as Kaiold picked up his plate, smashed the contents onto his neighbor's head and yelled, "Food Fight!"

Spurred by the Paranoy's actions, the food war quickly

spread through the cafeteria. Reaching the table I had been sitting at, the guards tried to locate me in the chaos, but it was no use—I was already long gone.

On the Run

Dodging patrols that were after my blood, I sneaked through the Academy. I knew I had to find Alyssa to clear my name, but quite frankly, I wasn't sure how to proceed. Alyssa had disappeared sometime between dinner last night and the beginning of class this morning, a period of nearly fourteen hours! That was a lot of time, during which the Zandu girl could have done nearly anything.

As a result, my best bet would be to check her room. The Academy had a strict 10 p.m. curfew, so unless Alyssa had been abducted before that point in time, she'd probably spent at least some time in bed.

Sneaking into the Academy Dormitories, I searched for the Zandu's room. As my quarters were way down at the far end of the building, I'd never been this way, so I had no idea how far I needed to go to find what I was looking for.

For close to fifteen minutes I looked unsuccessfully but then, right near the end of the hall, I found the room I was searching for. Quickly scanning the hallway to make sure I was alone, I sneaked into the room and closed the door.

I'd been worried that this search would be fruitless, but to my surprise, I discovered that the entire room had been trashed! All of Alyssa's lockers had been torn open, and the items of furniture in the room—a bed, a pair of chairs and a small table—had been broken to pieces and scattered across the floor.

Searching through the debris, I suddenly noticed a splotch of bright red smeared across the floor. Bending down to study it closer, I realized with horror that it was blood!

For a second, I feared that Alyssa had been killed, but then I remembered that Zandu blood is green, not red. This meant that the blood was from one of her attackers.

Before I could ponder this further, however, I suddenly heard the sound of voices coming down the hall. "…he might have returned to the scene of the crime?" someone was saying.

"I don't know," the other replied, "But we'd better check the girl's room just in case. Criminals do crazy things, after all."
My mouth dropped in shock. They were coming here! Desperate, I looked around, trying to find a place to hide. Unfortunately, the room was relatively Spartan in décor, and what little it had possessed was now in a heap on the floor.

The voices continued to get closer as I vainly searched, and I was on the verge of giving up when a soft voice whispered, "Jayden, up here!"

Looking up, I saw Nazo (the Schaddo I'd seen on my

first day) perched inside a ventilation shaft that ran above the room's ceiling. "What…" I began.

"No time to talk," he broke in, "You need to get out of there!" Reaching down, he added, "Give me your hand!" I did as he said, and with a surprising amount of strength for such a skinny being, Nazo hauled me off the floor and into the shaft overhead.

As soon as I was inside, the Schaddo slid a metal grate over the opening in the shaft, hiding any evidence as to where I'd gone. "Now come on!" my rescuer whispered, crawling off down the shaft. "We need to get out of here!"

Following the tall, thin alien through the Academy's ventilation system for several minutes, we finally arrived at a small room tucked deep within the space station. After checking to make sure we were alone, Nazo said, "We need to talk."

"Well, thanks for the rescue…" I began but was quickly interrupted.

"No, not about that," the Schaddo shook his head. "We need to speak about the kidnapping." After a dramatic pause, he continued, "I know who did it."

"Who was it?" I asked, ecstatic that I was about to be cleared.

Pausing for a moment to look me in the eye, Nazo

finally declared, "It was you."

Sub-Solar Secrets

For several moments following this accusation, I just gaped at the Schaddo, startled by his accusation. Eventually, however, I managed to say, "But it wasn't me!"

"I know," Nazo replied cryptically. Thoroughly confused, I stayed quiet as the Schaddo continued, "Last night around midnight, I was returning to my quarters when I suddenly heard the sounds of a struggle from inside one of the nearby rooms. I thought about investigating, but then the room's door flew open, and you came out, dragging an unconscious Alyssa behind you!"

"I was hoping you'd run upon seeing that there was a witness to your crime," Nazo continued. "But instead, you instantly went on the attack. I'm a good fighter, but you were on another level. It took all my skill to disengage."

"Wait for a second," I broke in, having spotted a weakness in the Schaddo's argument. "I'm not a strong fighter."

"I know," Nazo replied, "Which is why I'm talking to you right now. Someone is impersonating you, and I want to know why."

"I...don't know," I told him after a second. I mean, there

was that one thing, but…

Sensing the hesitation in my voice, the Schaddo asked, "What? What aren't you saying?"

"When I was confronted by Tykvas today, he gave me a ransom note that I'd supposedly written," I told my inquisitor. "In it, 'I' told the Zandu to leave the Earth alone. I had no idea why I'd say something like that, but then Kaiold (my Paranoy friend) said something about a sub-something…"

"The Sub-Solar Installation!" Nazo declared.

"Yes, that's it!" I told him. "So, what is it?"

"The Sub-Solar Installation is a space station that the Zandu constructed in your star system," the tall, thin alien explained. "Using special heat-resistant materials unique to the Zandu System, its orbit is so close to your sun to render it virtually unnoticeable. No one knows if it exists, but conspiracy theorists are adamant as to its existence."

"But why would the Zandu have a space station in the Earth's solar system?" I asked, perplexed.

"The Zandu don't trust the humans," Nazo told me. "They know the humans have adapted quickly and they fear that once the humans have become their technological equals, the humans will attempt to conquer the Zandu. The conspiracy theorists believe—and I concur—that the Sub-Solar Installation is a giant cannon."

"So if the humans grow too powerful," I realized, "The Zandu can end the threat with the push of a button."

"Exactly," the Schaddo nodded. "This means that whoever was impersonating you is probably trying to force a reaction from the Zandu. Most likely, they want the Zandu to destroy the Earth."

"But who'd want that?" I asked, perplexed. "We're new to the Galactic Alliance—we haven't had time to create any grudges with other races."

"In that case," Nazo replied, "We'll have to think outside the box. What if all this is a way of striking at the Zandu."

"You mean, by kidnapping the daughter of their most important Warlord?"

"Yes, but there's more than that," the tall, thin alien told me as he paced back and forth, clearly focused on the problem facing us. "Suppose the Zandu destroy the Earth using a secret space station hidden next to the planet's sun. Not only will they be heavily penalized for killing off a member of the Galactic Alliance, but they will have alienated the rest of the members. After all, would you be friends with someone who could have a world-shattering weapon pointed at your home planet?"

I had to admit, Nazo had a good point. The Zandu was

currently one of the more influential members of the Galactic Alliance—if they committed a travesty like this, it would destroy their reputation forever.

"So," Nazo began, "The question we have to ask is: who stands to gain from the fall of the Zandu?"

"Not only that," I added, "But we also need to figure out how they managed to make it look like I was the one committing the crime. They weren't shape-shifters, so some high-tech device…"

"That's it!" Nazo exclaimed. "It has to be the Changelings!"

"The who?"

"The Changelings," Nazo repeated. "One of the strangest races in the galaxy, the Changelings have the ability to change their appearance completely. Their home planet is in the Zandu system, and for as long as anyone can remember they've had an intense hatred for their more powerful neighbors."

"Great!" I declared. "We have a suspect, a motive and an idea of the villain's endgame. What's next?"

"Now," the Schaddo replied, "We have to save the girl, and fortunately for you, I know exactly where she is."

Rescue Operations

According to Nazo, the Changeling had taken Alyssa to a supply locker in an old, forgotten section of the space station. I'd wondered why the Schaddo hadn't just rescued her if he knew where she'd been taken, but then Nazo explained that the door had been programmed to only open for a specific DNA pattern. His hadn't worked, but he guessed that mine might since the Changeling had been using my skin during the kidnapping.

I agreed that it was worth a shot, so together we set off for the space station's upper deck where the locker was located. I thought it'd be safer to travel through the ventilation shafts, but the ventilation systems for the area around the locker were completely separate from the ones in the main station, so we had to walk instead. Fortunately, Nazo was an expert at the unseen movement, so even though we came within ten feet of several patrols, we managed to get through the main corridors without being spotted.

Thirty minutes of walking later, we arrived at a large metal door that was inscribed "Danger! Do not enter!" I turned to ask my companion about this, but before I could say a word, he handed me a bulky space-suit and said, "To save on energy, the Academy decided to de-pressurize the next section. Put this on, unless you want to explore the second the door is opened."

Taking the proffered suit, I slipped inside, asking, "If that's the case, how is Alyssa alive?"

"The Changeling sealed her inside a stasis pod he must have stolen from a medical station. She can survive indefinitely in there, as long as it isn't...accidentally...opened."

Understanding what the Schaddo was implying, I locked my helmet on and said, "Well, in that case, we'd better get going!" Nazo opened the door, and with a confident stride, I stepped into the old station...only to be propelled skyward by my first step.

"By the way," my companion called out over our in-suit radios, "The artificial gravity for this section has been turned off. Watch your step!"
"Thanks for the warning," I replied as my head gently bumped against the ceiling. I'd spent a little bit of time in the Academy's zero-gravity chamber, but there you had handholds everywhere to help keep your balance. Here, in a completely uncontrolled environment, things were going to be much more difficult.

Carefully pushing off from the ceiling, I flew through the air and crashed into the floor, sending reverberations of pain surging through my body. "Jayden, pull yourself along the wall using the support pillars," Nazo told me. "It's the only way to get anywhere in zero-grav."

Gritting my teeth against the pain, I reached out and latched onto the nearest pillar. "Well, here goes nothing," I muttered, and with a soft tug I pulled myself forward.

I was expecting to go shooting down the hallway like a human rocket, but instead gently floated away from the wall as if propelled by a soft, summer breeze. "Good job," Nazo's voice told me. "It looks like you're getting the hang of this. Now, take a left at the upcoming intersection."

Making sure to stay close to the wall, I did as he said, turning into another, even darker corridor. Up ahead, I could make out Nazo's form standing beside a large metal doorway with a DNA scanner on the wall nearby. "Is this it?" I asked upon arriving a minute later.

Nazo nodded and said, "Hold out your hand. The scanner will sync with your space suit to check your DNA against the DNA contained in the scanner. If your DNA matches, the door will open, and Alyssa will be saved."

Doing as the Schaddo said, I extended my hand. A couple of seconds passed, then a hatch on the DNA scanner opened and a metal probe popped out and hooked into a port on the wrist of my space suit. Beeping, the little device scanned my body for a moment before disconnecting and retracting back into the wall.

"New template accepted," a disembodied female voice declared, "Door will now open." With a soft click, the metal door receded into the ceiling, revealing a small room with a stasis chamber inside. Cautiously pulling myself into the room, I peered through the small window of the pod, letting out a sigh of relief. Alyssa was inside, and she was alive.

As I turned around to tell Nazo the good news, however, my body suddenly toppled out of the air and slammed into the ground. A second later, the corridor was flooded with light, and a hissing filled the air as the area was pressurized and oxidized.

"What…" I began, but then I saw Nazo, and my jaw dropped. The Schaddo had removed his helmet, but the face beneath was my face! "You're the Changeling!" I exclaimed in shock.

"Guilty as charged," the alien replied. "And now, you've fallen right into my trap!"
With horror, I realized that he was right. Not only had I run away from the Academy's guards, but now I was standing right beside the kidnapped Zandu, and my DNA was programmed into the door! Speaking of which… "The door said 'New template accepted' when it got my DNA," I told the Changeling. "That means that there hadn't been any DNA programmed into it beforehand!"

"Exactly," the villain replied with a mocking laugh. "But now, that's no longer true."

It was a very well-executed plot, but there was still one thing I didn't get. "What do you have to gain in all this," I asked. "Do you just want me to be arrested?"

"Oh, no," the Changeling shook his head. "You see, Alyssa isn't the only thing in that stasis chamber. She's sharing the pod with a fusion bomb."

My jaw dropped in horror as I realized what the villain was planning. "Let me guess," I broke in. "When the chamber is opened, it will explode, vaporizing Alyssa and everything else within thirty feet."

"Exactly," my foe replied. "Of course, the girl's father will want revenge so that the Earth will be destroyed within hours."

I was horrified by this announcement, but at the same time, I could see a giant hole in his plan. "One problem," I told him. "This bomb will probably kill lots of beings who aren't Zandu. If that happens, the public backlash against the Zandu for destroying Earth will be greatly decreased."

"It would be," the Changeling agreed, "If it wasn't discovered shortly afterward that you'd been framed, and that Tykvas Shak'zar was the one responsible for his sister's kidnapping and death."

"Let me guess," I said, "The convicting evidence will come from you?"
"Of course," the villain nodded in agreement. "And I'll also be the one that causes the suspect's 'accidental' death. This will prevent the Zandu from proving the boy's innocence, and public opinion will quickly turn against them."

Several moments of silence passed after the Changeling made this statement, as I attempted to process all this. "Well," I finally said, "That's a very good plan. There's just one thing in your way."

"And that is?"

I'd been quietly slipping out of my space suit as the villain talked, so when I rose to my feet, I was unencumbered by the bulky contraption. "I'm still here to stop you," I replied in a firm voice.

"You can try," the Changeling said, lunging forward.

The Imposter Revealed

Watching as the Changeling charged at me, I waited until the last second to nimbly leap out of his way. Still dressed in his bulky space suit, he was unable to correct his course in time, and whiffing right past me he slammed into the nearest wall.

Grunting in pain, the villain spun around, his face contorted with rage. "I'll get you!" he roared, sprinting toward me once more. Once again, I jumped out of the way at the last second, but this time he was ready, and with a powerful crash the two of us went down.

Rolling across the floor, we punched at each other, desperately seeking some advantage. The Changeling was a better fighter, but since he was encumbered by his space suit, I had an edge.

Realizing this, the Changeling suddenly morphed into a long, thin snake-like form! Startled, I jumped back, giving the creature enough time to slither out of the space suit. Once the Changeling had completely cleared the bulky outfit, he reformed, this time in the image of Nazo.

"There," the Changeling stated, "That's much better. Human bodies are so frail, so inelegant."

"Stop talking and fight me," I growled, putting up my fists. Honestly, I didn't have much hope—I wasn't the pinnacle of human fitness, and even if I was, there was no way I could take down a Schaddo.

Grinning, the Changeling leaped for me, but suddenly, a loud voice yelled, "Stop!" Freezing, the two of us spun to face the newcomer, but when I saw who it was my jaw dropped in horror.

Standing less than fifteen feet away, and surrounded by eight armed guards, was none other than Garamak Shak'zar! Too stunned to speak, I was unable to react when the Changeling said, "Warlord Shak'zar, I've found your daughter!"

"Really?" the Warlord asked. "You must be the one who contacted me."

My opponent nodded. "She's in a stasis pod in the storage locker over there. The Terran here is the kidnapper, and he was trying to kill me before I could tell you!"

Nodding, the Zandu ordered, "Guards, see if the Schaddo is telling the truth!" A pair of soldiers entered the locker, and after a second of examination, they confirmed the Changeling's story.

Watching as the guards tugged the stasis pod out of the narrow room, the Warlord declared, "Open it!"

Realizing that I couldn't wait any longer, I called out, "Stop; it's a trap!" The guards froze, and I continued,

"Sir, the Schaddo is lying. I didn't kidnap your daughter—he did. He's the one who placed the girl in that chamber, and he's the one who rigged the pod to explode if it was ever opened."

Upon hearing these words, the guards surrounding the pod jumped back in shock. Warlord Shak'zar, however, was unmoved. "Why would a Schaddo kidnap my daughter?" he asked.

"Because it's not a Schaddo at all," I replied. "It's a Changeling."

I was expecting this declaration to seal the deal in my favor, but instead, the Warlord just laughed. "A Changeling," he said, "Is that the best you can come up with?"

Desperately searching my mind for any proof I had to support my case, I thought about the moment I'd first met the Changeling. I was in Alyssa's room, and the floor was covered with…that's it!

Leaping for the Changeling, I scraped my fingernails across his face. Crying out in pain, my foe pressed a hand to the wound, but not before a little bit of green blood had seeped out. "Look at that," I told the Warlord. "Schaddo blood is red. This is no Schaddo."

His ruse exposed, the Changeling grabbed a lever on the back of Alyssa's stasis pod. "Drop your weapons or I blow her up!" he snarled, clearly not afraid to back up his threat.

Realizing they had no choice, the guards dropped their weapons. "Now drop your weapons and leave!" the Changeling ordered. Once again, the guards were forced to comply.
Snatching a pistol from the ground and pointing it at Garamak, the villain declared, "Warlord Shak'zar: you have oppressed my people for the last time! Now, without your guards to protect you, you will face justice!"

Realizing I had to act, I snatched a pistol from the floor and, in a single, smooth motion, I fired at the Changeling's head.

Vindicated

It took several hours for the Academy Bomb Squad to defuse the explosives contained inside Alyssa's stasis pod, but eventually, the Zandu girl was awakened. She appeared to be none the worse for wear, and after a quick check-up, the Academy Doctor confirmed this impression.

I'd been hoping to talk to her when she came out of stasis, but her father had insisted she stay in her room to recover. As a result, I just had to spend my time regaling my friends with tales of my heroism and valor.

When I told the real Nazo about his doppelganger, he merely laughed. "A Changeling tried to imitate me? Pathetic."

I'd laughed at the time, but he had a point. I'd fallen for the Changeling's story hook, line, and sinker, even though in hindsight, it wasn't that plausible. I quickly realized that I'd have to pick up the pace if I was ever going to do well here.

On the plus side, though, I was completely exonerated of the crime. Not only that but as a reward for the service I'd done, Warlord Shak'zar even promised to remove the Sub-Solar Installation!

In general, things had turned out well, but there was one aspect of the whole adventure that was still bugging me.

When I had found the blood in Alyssa's room, I'd assumed it belonged to her kidnapper. That wasn't possible, however, as the Changeling's blood was green (as I'd pointed out pretty obviously).

Something was going on here, and I'd never been able to rest until I got to the bottom of it.

Part Two: War Games

"Hah! Take that, Jayden!" Kaiold cried, peppering me with bullets from his assault rifle. Grunting from the force of the impacts, I quickly checked my shields. They were holding for the time being, but if I didn't get to safety soon, I'd fall prey to his incessant assault.

Firing a quick burst of plasma to cover my retreat, I darted through a nearby doorway. This seemed to annoy the Paranoy, who called out, "You can run, but you can't hide Terran! I'll get you!"

Ignoring the thin green alien's threats, I sprinted through the hallways of the dank building I'd just entered. The situation looked dire, but as long as I was out of the Paranoy's line of sight, I had a—

Blam! I was slammed in the stomach with the force of a freight train, knocking me to the floor. Curling up in agony, I could only watch as my assailant—a miniscule alien covered with green fur and brandishing a sniper rifle—stepped from the shadows. "Gotcha!" it squealed with excitement.

I attempted to reply, but it was too late—the world darkened, and massive red words proclaimed, "You have died – Respawning in 10...9...8..."

Sighing in frustration, I slumped back in my seat. Space Raider was one of the best vid-games in the galaxy, but it was also incredibly challenging for newbies. Hitting the chat button on my headset, I asked, "Jonk, how long have you been sitting there waiting for me?"

"Oh, not that long," the shrill-voiced Bangori replied.

"He's lying," Kaiold told me matter-of-factly. "He's been there all game."

"How would you know...?" I began, then paused. "Kaiold, are you map-hacking again?"

"Me?" the Paranoy asked, deeply wounded by my accusation. "You think I'd be map-hacking?"

"Um, sorry to break in," a melodious female voice declared, "But what exactly is map-hacking?"

Recognizing the speaker as Alyssa Shak'zar, a small smile crossed my face. Alyssa was supposedly the daughter of a Zandu Warlord, but—at least in my opinion—her pale skin and braided brown hair looked more Terran than Zandu. "Map-hacking," I replied, "Is when a player uses a program to hack into a vid-game's data and figure out where all his opponents are. This lets him avoid ambushes and take out his foes with impunity."

"So that's how he's beating me!" Alyssa exclaimed. "I knew it!"

Hitting a button on my controller, I quickly checked the stats. So far in this match, Alyssa had died nearly fifty times, while Kaiold only had twenty-three kills. I was about to point this fact out to the Zandu girl, then I thought better of it and simply replied, "Yep, that's it."

As I hit the button to respawn, I marveled at how universal vid-games were. Nearly every race played them, and for the most part, they all liked the exact same things: action, adventure, and a great story. (There are a couple of races that like social games revolving around farming of all things, but we aren't going to mention them).

Unfortunately, galactic vid-gaming has its share of cheaters as well, and Kaiold was definitely one of them. "Kaiold, you need to stop map-hacking right now," I told the Paranoy player. "Unless you want me to report you...again."
"Your threats don't scare me, Terran," Kaiold replied with a laugh. "After all, you have no proof."

I opened my mouth to contradict his statement, but then I paused. To tell the truth, he was right. Every time I tried to report the Paranoy to the Principal, I was told that I needed more evidence before I could make an accusation like that.

Sighing, I was about to go back to the game when I

suddenly thought of something. Kaiold was using his map-hacking program right now, so if I could hack into the game's source code and locate the program, I'd be able to bust the Paranoy once and for all!

Hiding my character in a far corner of the map, I quickly typed in a cheat code that replaced the game-screen with an image of the source code. Scrolling down to the section concerning map-creation, I began searching for Kaiold's program.

Before attending the Galactic Academy, I'd been planning to pursue a career in programming vid-games. As a result, it didn't take my trained eye long to find the inconsistencies in Space Raider's original coding. The added commands were surprisingly crude, and after copying the segment for proof, it only took a couple of keystrokes to return the game to the way it was meant to be played.

Smiling at Kaiold's sudden cry of outrage upon realizing what I'd done, I was about to shut down the source code when I suddenly noticed another little bug in the coding. It was tucked into the section regarding scoring, and at a glance, it appeared to allow players to gain bonus points for specific types of kills.

"So map-hacking wasn't enough, eh?" I muttered, deleting the code. "That will show you…" Suddenly, the source code window disappeared, and the screen went black.

"What on Earth…" I began, but then the screen popped

to life once more, displaying hundreds of rows and columns full of numbers. Thinking it was some stats list for the game's weapons, I scrolled to the top of the page, where a giant green banner said, "Intergalactic Bank of Financia—Online Edition."

Horrified, my mouth dropped in shock. I was looking at a bank account!

Thieves and Hackers

My mind racing, I tried to figure out what to do next. The Finans (a race of intergalactic bankers) worshiped money like a god, so hacking into someone's account at a Finan bank was a crime frequently punished by death. I really didn't want to die this young, so perhaps the best course of action would be to shut this page down and pretend I never saw it.

Just as I was about to do this, however, a thought crossed my mind. Whoever owned this account had gone to a lot of trouble to hide it in the code for Space Raider. That likely meant that they were doing something illegal, which I should be able to check pretty easily.

Deciding that another minute or two wouldn't hurt anything, I began snooping through the rows of numbers. Most of them seemed legitimate and pretty basic (small salary deposits, a couple of payments for utility bills and food) but then, about three-fourths of the way down the page, I found what I was looking for.

Whoever owned the account had received a payment for nearly fifty-thousand Finars, which is equivalent to about five million Terran Dollars. This was crazy enough, but then I saw who the payment was from, and my jaw nearly fell off my face in shock.

The money had come from the Galactic Academy!

Scrolling down the page, I saw another, similar payment less than twenty rows down. This pattern continued all the way down the page, and the current balance line at the bottom showed a sum of nearly 2 million Finars!

Clearly, someone had been stealing from the Galactic Academy—the only questions were who the thief was, and how they were pulling off this crime. Hoping for an easy break, I went to the account homepage, but where the owner's name should have been there was nothing.

Deciding that uncovering the villain's identity would have to wait, I exited out of the bank account and returned to the game code. The criminal had been tampering with the code for a reason—if I could find out why I'd be that much closer to uncovering the truth.

Hitting the undo button to return the code to its previous appearance, I intensely studied the suspect programming, searching for any devious purpose to the code. To my surprise, however, there was nothing, as the code merely referenced another file containing all scoring information.

Curious, I followed the link, where I found a page full of complex code. Even with my skill at coding, it took a while to decipher, but once I finished translating the commands, I realized that I had discovered the criminal's secret.

Using the Space Raider as a front, the thief had been covertly hacking into the Academy's financial accounts to siphon out funds. It was a truly ingenious way to commit this theft because it only made the network connection when the game was running. If it were shut down, the thief's connection to the account would be severed without a trace, providing him with complete immunity to detection. It was only through blind luck that I'd stumbled upon his secret—now; the only question was what to do with this information.

As I considered this, a voice suddenly boomed over my headphones, "Jayden, are you still playing?"

Startled by Kaiold's sudden question, it took a moment for me to reply, "Yeah, of course. Why are you asking?"

"Because I haven't seen you in nearly ten minutes," the Paranoy told me. "And since my…location aid…isn't working anymore, I haven't been able to find you."
"Well, I've been a little busy," I said, trying to remain calm. The last thing I needed was for a blabbermouth Paranoy to tell the world that I was looking into a private account in a Finan Bank. "Who's winning now?" I asked, trying to change the subject.

"Me, of course…" Kaiold began, but he was quickly interrupted by Alyssa.
"No, you aren't," the Zandu girl declared. "Jonk's winning."

"Jonk's winning?" I asked, nearly falling out of my chair in surprise.

"Apparently," Kaiold declared in annoyance, "Jonk is a big-time Space Raider champion back on his homeworld."

"I wanted to play easily on you all," the Bangori squeaked, "But when Kaiold started cheating, I decided to show him a lesson."

Laughing at this completely deserved turnaround, I shut down the game code and returned to playing, unaware of the dark days that lay ahead.

The Announcement

My troubles began two days later. I was dissecting a Bangorian Tulok Lizard when Principal Jandork's voice suddenly declared over the PA system, "Students of the Galactic Academy—there is a criminal in your midst!"

Needless to say, this caused everyone to jump in their seats, but honestly, I was a bit relieved. I'd been dreading the time when I'd have to explain how I ended up looking at a Finan Bank Account; now, it appeared that time would never come.

"Yesterday," the Principal continued, "One of the Academy's computer experts discovered a discrepancy in the station's network hub. Looking into it, he discovered that someone had made an unauthorized connection to an outside source."

"He tried to isolate it further, but the hacker was smart, and had left no trail. As a result, I have decided to call on you students for help. If you have any information regarding this terrible crime, please let me or one of your teachers know."

"The penalty for any cybercrime is instant—and permanent—expulsion from the Academy," the Principal concluded, "So once this criminal is found they will come to justice!"

The PA system shut off abruptly, leaving the class in an uproar. Every student had a theory on who the hacker was, and they made sure to share their opinion with everyone else. I remained silent, however, frozen by the realization that the hacker they were referring to was me.

My crime hadn't been intentional, but it wouldn't matter; if anyone found out about what I'd done, I'd be done for. Even worse, however, was what this meant for my investigation. My only proof had been acquired through this "criminal act"—if I revealed what I knew, I'd be expelled, and no further investigation would occur. This meant that if the thief were to be stopped, I'd have to do it myself.

Unfortunately, I had no idea where to start. The only lead I had was the code, and now that a hacker alert had been put out, I wasn't going near that. This left me with only one option: talk to my friends.

As soon as class let out, I set off for the cafeteria where my friends and I often met after the morning classes. Thanks to the Principal's announcement, the room was a lot louder than normal, and upon entering I inadvertently cringed with guilt. Fortunately, no one noticed, and I was able to get my food without any trouble.

After a quick search of the cafeteria I located my friends and, quickly bracing myself for what lay ahead, I strode across the room and sat down at their table.

"Hey, Jayden," Kaiold greeted me as I sat down, "We were just talking about you!" Despite the fact that he'd been cheating in Space Raider, the Paranoy was still one of my friends. In fact, aside from Alyssa, he was probably my best friend.

"Really?" I asked, worried that they suspected my guilt. "What were you saying?"

"Kaiold here was telling us how bad you are at Space Raider," Alyssa told me, flashing me a bright smile. "I've been trying to clear up these lies, but so far I've had no luck."

Silently breathing a sigh of relief, I replied, "Well, he's not totally wrong—after all, compared to Jonk, I'm nothing."

Beka, Jonk's older sister, laughed at this. "You were playing against Jonk in Space Raider?" she asked in her high-pitched voice. "You know he's the best Bangori player ever, right?"

"So I've been told," I replied, chuckling.

Kaiold frowned as he replied, "So I don't check the Space Raider rankings for every planet. Sue me." Pausing for a moment, he added, "By the way, what do you guys think about the Principle's announcement this morning? Do you really think there's a hacker?"

I opened my mouth to speak, but Alyssa beat me to the punch, "Of course there is!" she told the Paranoy. "What, you think the Principal is lying?"

"Duh!" Kaiold replied, indignant at the Zandu's doubt. "He's a Principal! Not only that, but he's a Paranoy, like me! They always have ulterior motives for what they do."

Something about what Kaiold had just said struck me as odd, but before I could nail the feeling down Alyssa said, "I know a couple of Paranoy, so I'm pretty sure you're an exception to the rule."

Breaking in before this could get out of hand I said, "Stop this arguing! Whether or not the Principal is devious is irrelevant, because in this case I know he's telling the truth."

All my friends turned to face me in surprise as I finished, "I'm the hacker they're looking for."

Full Disclosure

This statement was greeted with several seconds of stunned silence, as my friends attempted to process my shocking announcement. Taking advantage of this pause, I said, "Kaiold's right, though—there is more to this than the Principal's letting on."

"I knew it!" the Paranoy declared, pumping his fist in triumph. "Let me guess: you're a member of the Terran resistance who is infiltrating the Academy to gain intelligence for your people. You got the necessary info, so you sent it out to your allies, but now…

"No," I stated flatly, "It's nothing like that."

"Okay, then," Kaiold replied thoughtfully, "I bet you're a cybernetic super-soldier who is planning to assassinate one of the staff. You weren't told beforehand who you were supposed to kill, so you have to connect to an outside relay to find out."

"No," I said again.

"Then you have to be a Changeling in disguise who—"

"No, no, no!" I exclaimed. "It's nothing like that at all!" Taking a second to calm down I said, "Remember two days ago when we were playing Space Raider, and you were map-hacking?"

Kaiold nodded as I continued, "I was getting fed up with your cheating, so I hid my character in a remote corner of the map and switched into the game code. It didn't take me long to find your addition to the programming, and after making a copy as evidence, I deleted the commands."

"So that was you!" the Paranoy exclaimed. "In that case, you should be punished for hacking my program."
"But that doesn't make any sense," Alyssa broke in. "The Principal said that the hacker connected to an outside source. The files that you changed in Space Raider were all located on computers within the Academy."

"You're correct," I told the Zandu. "What I did there wasn't against the rules. However, before I returned to the game, I decided to check around some more to see if you'd made any other…alterations to the code. After a few minutes, I found a couple of new commands in the section regarding scoring. I assumed you'd been the one who created them, so I immediately deleted them."

"But I didn't make any modifications to the scoring code!" Kaiold exclaimed, clearly confused.

"I know," I replied, "Because as soon as I cleared the commands, the screen suddenly transitioned to something completely different."

"What was it?" Jonk squeaked, echoing the sentiment the rest of my audience was clearly feeling.

"It was a Finan Bank Account," I stated grimly.

Kaiold's mouth dropped. "You hacked into a Finan Bank Account? You're crazier than I thought!"

"I didn't hack into it," I corrected, "I was redirected there from the game code."

"That's really weird," Alyssa interjected.

Nodding at her insight, I replied, "Exactly. In fact, it was so strange that I decided to quickly check out the account to make sure everything was on the level."

"And was it?"

"Not even close," I declared, shaking my head. "In the past couple months, the owner has received regular 50,000 Finar payments from the Galactic Academy! If that isn't a sign of thievery, nothing is!"

A chorus of agreements echoed from around the table. "Unfortunately," I continued, "The account's owner was anonymous, so I was unable to proceed without help. Originally I planned to tell the principal about what I'd found, but now I don't think that'll work too well."

"Let me guess," Kaiold interjected, "You want our help, right?"
I nodded. "I can't do this on my own," I told them, "And it's only a matter of time until someone discovers I was

the hacker. Please, you're my only chance to expose this crime!"

"Well, in that case," the Paranoy slowly replied, "I guess we have no choice…"

"What he means to say," Alyssa corrected, "Is that we'll be happy to help!"

"Perfect," I beamed broadly. "Meet me in the study hall after classes are over so we can go over plans." Pausing a moment for emphasis, I added, "If we all work together, this criminal stands no chance!"

Gathering Intelligence

Gathering in the study hall later that afternoon, we made our plans. Thanks to our technical knowledge, Kaiold and I were picked to go back into the code and search for clues. While we did that, Alyssa and the two Bangori would look for physical evidence that could possibly put us on the right track.

After about an hour of discussion, we broke up into groups and set off on our various missions. Alyssa, Beka, and Jonk went to the Academy's Records Office to check for evidence, while Kaiold and I went to the vid-gaming room to check out the code some more.

We knew it'd be a little risky to check the code in the public gaming room, but it was our only choice. If we worked out of our dorm rooms and accidentally triggered a firewall, the Academy's cyber-security squad would immediately know who to arrest. At least this way, we'd have some warning and a sense of anonymity.

Sitting down at a pair of consoles near the back of the room, Kaiold and I fired up a game of Space Raider. "So," the Paranoy asked, "What exactly are we looking for?"

"The commands added by the thief referenced another file, which contained the code used to transfer the funds. My hope is that between the two of us, we can figure out who created this document, or at the very least, where it came from."

"Because if we can do that," Kaiold realized, "Then finding the thief should be no problem."

"Exactly," I replied. "Now let's get to work."

Ducking into the game's source code, we quickly located the scoring section. I'd been a little worried that the Principal's announcement may have caused the thief to erase his work, but it appeared that greed had overwhelmed common sense, as the code was still there.

"Wow," Kaiold muttered upon seeing the added commands, "How on earth did I miss that when I was making my...adjustments?"

"You weren't looking for it," I replied. "I was deliberately searching for inconsistencies, and I still only barely noticed it."

"Well, one thing's for sure," the Paranoy declared as we returned to our work, "Whoever did this is a master hacker, with skill rivaling my own!"

"If that's all the skill he has," I chuckled softly, "Then we shouldn't have anything to worry about."

Opening up the file the commands referenced, we began studying the code before us. Because of the code's complexity, our progress was slow, and it wasn't until we were nearly half-way through the lengthy document that we had our first breakthrough.

In the section of the code dedicated to breaking through the Academy's firewall, we discovered a series of complex calculations designed to figure out the system's password. Many programs like that exist, but this one was incredibly precise as if the person who created it had an intimate knowledge of the firewall's password algorithm.

Picking up on this as well, Kaiold said, "You know what this means, right?"
"This was an inside job," I muttered.

"Not only that," the Paranoy corrected, "But the thief is a high-ranking member of the Academy. After all, they don't just give out their firewall codes to every janitor and teacher's assistant."

"So we know that the thief is an expert hacker and that he is likely a senior professor or an administrator at the Academy," I recapped. "We're not done yet, but it's definitely a good start!"

Exiting the game, we left the room. By now, Alyssa and the Bangori should have completed their part of the investigation and would be meeting us back in the study hall to compare our results. If their investigation had gone as well as ours, we could wrap this investigation up right now!

Arriving at the rendezvous point ten minutes later,

Alyssa and her team were nowhere to be seen. This wasn't too surprising, as the Records Office was on the far side of the Academy, so it'd take them a bit longer to get here.

When half an hour passed, however, and they still hadn't arrived, we began to suspect that something had gone terribly wrong. Deciding to investigate, we were about to head out when suddenly, the PA system activated and we heard the Principal's voice declare:

"Students of the Galactic Academy, I have great news for you: we have caught the hackers!"

"Well," Kaiold declared, "This can't be good."

Unlikely Allies

"Just fifteen minutes ago," Principal Jandork began, "Security guards caught three young students attempting to access secure files in the Academy Records Office. They were immediately taken into custody, where they quickly confessed to hacking our systems."

"Apparently," he continued, "They were using school computers to break into accounts at a Finan Bank, and if we hadn't caught them, they'd have pulled off the heist of the century."

Pausing several seconds to let this sink in, the Principal added, "In light of the nature of their crime—and at the request of the Finan members of the board—we've decided to change the punishment these students will receive. Tonight at supper, Alyssa Shak'zar, Beka and Jonk are going to be handed over to the Finan government, who will execute them publically!"

At this announcement, a roar of outrage tore through the entire Academy, as every student shouted their opinion of this travesty. Alyssa was well-liked and had a spotless reputation. No one in their right mind would accuse her of something like this!

Beka and Jonk were less well-known, but still, Bangori were famous for their intense dislike for criminal behavior. The only crime on their home world was caused by beings from other worlds; it made no sense that they'd be committing a crime here.

"You know what this means, of course," Kaiold told me. "They uncovered the truth, so whoever's behind the thefts had to get rid of them quickly."

Nodding, I replied, "In that case, we have no choice—we need to rescue them."
"But how?" Kaiold asked. "There's only two of us…"

"Don't worry about that," I broke in. "In fact, I can think of a couple of people who will be happy to help us. Come on, follow me."

Leaving the study hall, we returned to the vid-gaming room, where I found one of our potential recruits playing some virtual reality game. Waving to get his attention, I watched as he paused the game and walked over to where Kaiold and I were standing.

"Hey, Tykvas," I called out as he approached, "I need your help."

Like most Zandu, Tykvas Shak'zar was on the tall side, with purplish skin and spiky black hair. When I first arrived at the Academy, he was a little cold to me, but since I helped rescue his sister (read the story here), we'd become much better friends.

"Hello, Jayden," he greeted me softly, his face downcast. "Have you heard about Alyssa?"

Nodding, I replied, "That's why we're here. We believe—actually, we know—that Alyssa was framed, but unless we do something she's going to die for someone else's crimes. For us to pull off a rescue, however, we need allies."

"I'd be happy to help!" the Zandu declared a spark of hope in his eyes at the prospect of saving his sister. "What do you need?"

I opened my mouth to reply, but another voice broke in, "I also would like to help you." Turning in surprise, I saw Nazo—an alien of the Schaddo race—step out from the shadows behind us.

I'd had a couple of run-ins with the brooding Schaddo before, so this offer of help surprised me. "My people have protected the Bangori for generations," the newcomer continued, sensing my confusion. "It wouldn't be right for me to let them die like this."

"Well then," I told him, "We're glad to have you." The Schaddo were renowned for their skill as assassins, and Nazo was no exception. His addition to our little team gave us the wild-card that we so desperately needed.

"So," Tykvas asked, "What's the plan?"

Smiling deviously, I replied, "Okay, here's what we're going to do…"

Daring Rescue

The next hour was full of chaos, as we rushed around making sure everything was in place. My plan was a complex one, but if we were to rescue the prisoners, we'd need to do it quickly and quietly.

At the moment, Alyssa and the Bangori were being held in a high-security cell, but they were going to be handed over to the Finans at supper. This meant that our only chance for rescue would be while they were traveling between the two locations.

Using a map of the Academy that Nazo procured, we plotted out the routes that the prisoners were most likely to take. Discovering that there were only two possible paths, Nazo said that he would watch the convoy and tell us which way it was going.

In the meantime, the rest of us began mining both passageways with a vast assortment of booby-traps. None of them were lethal, but they would hinder the convoy enough to give the rest of my plan time to be executed.

Just as we finished setting up the final trap, my comm suddenly buzzed to life. "Jayden," Nazo's voice whispered in my ear, "They're heading out, and they're taking the southern corridor!"

A smile broke out across my face. The southern corridor

was much longer, and it ran right outside the Academy Dormitories, giving us the perfect opportunity for an ambush. "Great!" I exclaimed, "Now follow them and keep me posted on everything they do."

Turning to Tykvas and Kaiold, I declared, "They're taking the southern corridor—let's go!" Dashing over to the Dormitories, we all ducked into Tykvas's room and closed the door behind us.

Five minutes passed, then Nazo said, "They're entering the Dormitory corridor now, and will be at your position momentarily."

Thanking him, I turned to my team and asked, "Okay, team, do you all know what to do?" Everyone replied in the affirmative, so I continued, "Then get ready because it's show time."

Just as I finished speaking, there was a sudden "snap" from the hallway outside the room, and a guard yelled, "What in the universe? I just stepped in something...yaaaaah!" That was our signal, and flinging the door open the three of us leaped out into the hallway.

I'd been hoping that our traps would distract the guards somehow, but even in my wildest dreams, I'd never expected them to work this well. Apparently, the guards had all rushed forward to help their fallen comrade when he went down, and in their haste, they accidentally trapped themselves too.

Shaking my head in disbelief, I rushed over to where Alyssa and the Bangori were standing. Their faces were plastered with stunned expressions, but upon seeing us, they quickly broke out in smiles. "Jayden," Alyssa asked as I approached, "Did you do all this?"

"I had a little help," I replied, pointing over my shoulder at my allies, "But right now we don't have time for thanks. Those guards will free themselves any moment now, and if we're not gone by then, this whole operation will have been for naught."

Pulling an electro-knife from my pocket, I quickly sliced through the prisoners' bonds. "Now come on!" I yelled, "It's time to go!" Motioning for the rest to follow, I darted back into Tykvas's room.

As soon as I closed the door, the vent cover on the roof was pulled up, and Nazo's head poked through. "Up here," he called out, dropping a rope through the hole.

Struck by a sudden sense of déjà vu—a situation exactly like this had happened in my last adventure—I climbed up into the ventilation shaft. The others quickly joined me, and as soon as we were all up, the Schaddo slid the vent cover back into place, removing any trace of our escape.

Crawling on all fours, Nazo led us through the ventilation shafts to a large control room near the center of the station, and after quickly checking for any hidden microphones, he said, "It's all clear…you can talk now."

Nodding my thanks to the mysterious alien, I turned to Alyssa and asked, "So, Alyssa, what did you, and the Bangori find?"

"We found out who the thief is!" the Zandu girl exclaimed with excitement.
"And...?" I prompted.
"It's Principal Jandork!"

The Paranoy's Plan

When Alyssa made this announcement, the jaws of every being in the room dropped in unison. We'd known the thief was high-ranking, but we'd never expected him to be this high. "How do you know?" I eventually asked.

"While we were searching the Records Office," Alyssa replied, "Principal Jandork suddenly came in. He was clutching a thick datapad in his hand, and he was nervously scanning the room as if he were afraid that someone would see him."

"This seemed suspicious to me, so I made sure to keep an eye on him as he walked over to a large console and plugged the datapad in for a file transfer. Before it could be completed, however, someone called his name from the room's entrance, and Jandork walked over, leaving the datapad unattended."

"Deciding to see what the Principal was up to, I crept over and took a look," the Zandu girl continued. "It took a moment for me to understand what I was seeing, but then it hit me—the Principal was downloading a virus into the firewall!"

As she said this, a wave of realization suddenly hit me. "He was trying to erase his tracks!" I exclaimed. "The virus would have completely destroyed the firewall, which would get rid of any evidence that he was behind the thefts!"

Alyssa nodded. "I was going to get a picture, but before I could, Jandork spotted me and called in Security. With the Bangori's help, I tried to fend off the attackers, but there were too many of them, and we were quickly overwhelmed."

"And we know the rest of the story," I told her, "So that just leaves us with the question of what to do now."

Kaiold had been unusually quiet for this whole time, but now he broke in and declared, "Guys, I have a plan!"

***

Fifteen minutes later, we found ourselves outside the Principal's office. I was incredibly nervous...after all, if Kaiold's plan didn't work, we'd certainly be executed. "Okay, everyone," the Paranoy declared with an encouraging smile, "Just let me do all the talking." Nodding mutely, I watched as he walked up to the office's imposing door and called out, "Principal Jandork, I need to speak to you!"

Several seconds passed, then the door slid open with a silent hiss. Taking a couple of breaths to calm our nerves, the six of us walked through the door and into the office beyond.

When we first entered, the Principal was busy reading something on his datapad, but upon seeing who his visitors were, he dropped the device in shock. "Alyssa,

Beka, Jonk—you're supposed to be dead!"

"A fate which doesn't seem to worry you," Kaiold declared.

"They're criminals," the Principal replied. "They deserve to be punished."

"I agree," my friend nodded, "Criminals should be punished." Pausing a second for emphasis, he added, "So why don't you just give yourself up right now?"

At first, Jandork had no reply to this, but then his mouth tightened into a snarl, and he growled, "So, the Zandu told you, eh? Well, no matter—my virus is destroying the Academy's firewall as we speak, erasing any evidence of my wrongdoing. Soon, no one will know that I've been stealing money from the Academy, and…"

"We'll know," Kaiold broke in. "After all, you just told us your plans."

"I did, didn't I?" the Principal asked, casually reaching beneath his desk. "Well then, I guess I just need to make you all…disappear." In a flash, he brought his hand back up, and to our horror, we saw that he had a plasma pistol clutched within his fist.

"You know," he told us, pointing the weapon in our direction, "It didn't have to be like this. If you'd restrained your curiosity and hadn't investigated, none of this would ever have happened. I wouldn't have sent your friends to be executed, and I wouldn't have to shoot you now."

"Oh, you won't be shooting us," Kaiold told him confidently. Scowling evilly, Jandork was about to prove my friend wrong when suddenly, a dark figure dropped through a hole in the ceiling and tackled the principal to the ground.

"Heh, pathetic," Nazo declared, standing above the villain's prone form. "For a race that once dedicated themselves to stopping assassins like me, you've sure fallen a long way."

"Thanks for the save," Kaiold told the newcomer. "Did you get what we need?"
"Here it is," the Schaddo replied, handing my friend a small camera. "Principal Jandork's full confession."

"Well, what do you know?" Kaiold said, clearly more than a little surprised. "My plan worked!"

All's Well...

When the Academy Guards arrived five minutes later, they initially tried to arrest us for attacking the Principal and causing general disruption. After Kaiold presented the confession Nazo had recorded, however, the scene changed drastically.

Jandork was immediately taken into custody, and the orders for the capture of Alyssa and the Bangori were rescinded. In fact, the Academy issued formal apologies to the three wronged students and the Finans who were going to be my friend's executioners instead paid them large amounts of money to keep quiet about the whole affair.

As for me, I was just happy that it was all over. The last several days had been terrible for me since I was in constant fear of being revealed as the hacker. Now that the real villain had been uncovered, however, I was free to go about my normal life.

Two days after the Principal had been shipped away to the highest-security prison in the galaxy, I found myself back in the Academy's vid-gaming room, playing Space Raider with my friends. Without the help of a map-hacking program, Kaiold had reverted back to our level, and the game was surprisingly even, with no clear advantage being gained by any player.

After one especially intense firefight, I was in the

process of retreating back to my base when I was suddenly tapped on the shoulder. Turning, I saw Alyssa standing beside me, a small smile on her beautiful face. "Jayden," she told me, "I wanted to thank you for rescuing me."

"Oh, really, it was nothing," I told her. "You're my friend—I couldn't let you die. Besides," I pointed back at the screen, "You're my best source of points in this game."

"In that case," the Zandu replied with a laugh, "I'd best get back to that." Returning to the game as she walked away, a smile broke out on my face as I realized that even if I faced a hundred more challenges over the course of my time at the Academy, my friends would always have my back...

..well, except for when they were shooting at it.

Part Three: The New Student

"No, Alyssa, you need to turn the hydro-wrench clockwise to tighten the bolt," I declared, softly grabbing the Zandu girl's hand to guide her actions.

"Are you sure?" she asked, turning to look at me. "I thought the instructor said that turning the bolt right would tighten it."

"Right is clockwise," I replied, shaking my head. "Here, let me show you." Taking the tool from Alyssa's hand, I quickly tightened the bolt, sighing in exasperation. When I'd first heard that Alyssa and I were going to be partners for a class on mechanics, I was excited. We were great friends, so if we worked together, we'd be able to complete all our studies with ease.

Unfortunately, I hadn't taken into account how hopeless the Zandu girl was at anything related to machining. She didn't know the difference between electro-pliers and a screwdriver, so anything she worked on was destined for a terrible end. This was only our first class, but I was already on the verge of doing something drastic.

"Oh, so that's how it goes!" Alyssa exclaimed, examining my handiwork. "I never would have guessed!"

I was about to give her a scathing reply, but then the PA system turned on, and a voice declared, "Jayden Armstrong, your services are required in the hanger bay immediately."

"Why would they need you?" Alyssa asked, a confused look on her face.

"I have no idea," I replied, just as surprised as she was. I couldn't think of anything I'd be needed for in the hanger—I wasn't a pilot, after all—but if the mysterious voice on the PA system said I was needed, I had no choice but to go.

"I should be right back," I told Alyssa, rising from my seat. "Don't touch anything."

"Yes, sir," the Zandu girl replied, giving me a mock salute. "I shall wait eagerly for your return."
Chuckling, I left the classroom and jogged in the direction of the hanger. Reaching the large room a minute later, I entered just in time to see a massive spacecraft set down on the main landing pad.

The ship had a sleek, polished exterior and was constructed from a white metal that I'd never seen before. Its design didn't match any race I knew of, so I was interested to see who these newcomers were.

A couple of minutes passed, then the ship's hatch slowly

opened, and a pair of figures stepped out. They were both females, with long, blonde hair and skin that was so pale it appeared to be transparent. I'd never seen any beings like them before, so I was unsure how to approach this situation.

Fortunately, this problem was taken care of, since upon reaching the floor of the hanger, the taller of the two beings turned to me and said, "Hello, Jayden Armstrong, it is good to meet you. I am Elise, and this is my daughter Karia."

Her voice was melodious and pure, but it was something else about her greeting which caught my attention. "How…how do you know my name?" I stammered, my shock at this fact overwhelming everything else.

"It's pinned on your shirt," Karia declared, pointing a delicate finger at the name-tag attached to my chest. The girl's voice was less refined than that of her mother, and beneath her calm demeanor, I could sense an independent spirit attempting to break out.

"You appear to be wondering why we're here," Elise broke in, clearly sensing my confusion. "Well, I'll tell you: two days ago, the Galactic Council chose me to be the new Principal of the Galactic Academy. They didn't state all their reasons, but I believe a big one is the fact that I'm a Kelian, and we are above petty things such as greed and thievery."

I had to agree that Elise's hiring made sense, as the

previous Principal—a Paranoy named Jandork—had stolen a huge quantity of the Academy's money. (Read all about it in my previous book!) If Elise was truly as virtuous as she claimed, then the Academy shouldn't have to worry about trouble from that side.

Still, there was one thing I didn't understand, and raising my hand I asked, "So, that's great and all, but why exactly am I here?"

"Two reasons," Elise replied with a vague smile. "First, I wanted to see the student who was responsible for my predecessor's demise."

"And...?"

"You don't seem like you'll be much trouble, but I'll be keeping an eye on you. As for the second thing," the Kelian woman continued, "I'd like you to show my daughter around the Academy."

"Why me?" I asked.

"Because you're here, for one thing," Elise replied. "But also, my daughter has always wanted to meet a Terran. This way, she can get her wish."

"I see," I replied. "Well, in that case, let me be the first to welcome the two of you to the Galactic Academy! I hope you'll enjoy your time here."

"Oh, I will," Karia whispered, in a soft voice so low I

barely heard it. "I definitely will."

Sparks Fly

For the next hour or so, I gave Karia a tour of the school, pointing out everything of note. The young Kelian nodded with interest at everything I showed her, but at the same time, she seemed distracted, as if her mind were in another place.

"And this," I told her, gesturing to a nearby door, "Is the Academy's machine shop."

"What kind of things do you do in there?" Karia asked curiously, her beautiful voice laden with interest.

"All kinds of things," I replied with a smile. "In fact, just before you arrived, I was working on a school project with my friend Alyssa. Now that I mention it," I added after a moment, "I should probably go check to see how Alyssa is doing."

Motioning for the pretty Kelian to follow, I opened the door of the machine shop and stepped inside. Upon seeing what Alyssa had done to our project, however, I let out a slight gasp of shock.

When I'd left the room, the scale model of a Zandu Battlecruiser had been less than halfway done, but now it was nearly complete. "Alyssa?" I called out, and a familiar face popped up from the far side of the model. "Did you do all this?"

The girl nodded proudly, "You bet. Do you like it?"

"But...how?" I asked, shaking my head in disbelief. "When we were working together earlier, you showed a complete lack of any mechanical ability."

"Oh, that was just an act," Alyssa explained. "I just enjoyed watching your growing frustration at my 'ineptitude'."

"I see," I replied, a mock frown on my face. "So, is it done?"

"Just about," the Zandu replied. "By the way," she added, noticing my companion for the first time. "Who's the girl with you?"

"This is Karia," I told my friend. "She's a Kelian."

"Hello, Karia," Alyssa exclaimed, extending her hand. "I'm Alyssa Shak'zar."
"Shak'zar," the young Kelian repeated as she took the proffered hand. "That sounds like a Zandu name, but you're a Terran."

"I'm not a Terran!" Alyssa declared, her face flushed. "Why does everyone make this mistake?"

"Probably because you look like a Terran, you talk like a Terran, and you spend time with Terrans," Karia replied. "To tell the truth, I don't see any trace of Zandu in you."

Trying to head them both off before they could descend into violence, I broke in and said, "Girls, girls, calm down. Karia, how many Zandu have you met?"

"None, I suppose," the Kelian muttered. "But in the holo-vids, they…"

"Holo-vids don't always depict reality," I replied. "In fact, the events they contain are almost always completely made up."

Alyssa looked like she was about to inject her two cents into the conversation as well, but then the strangest thing happened. The Zandu Battlecruiser model that we'd been working on earlier suddenly fell off its stand and crashed to the ground, scattering pieces everywhere.

"What in the galaxy?" Alyssa exclaimed, jumping back in surprise. "I'm sure I mounted it to the stand."

Groaning, I fell to my knees, watching as hours of work slowly rolled across the room's floor. A second passed, then to my surprise, a soft hand came to rest on my shoulder. "Don't worry, Jayden," Karia's smooth voice whispered in my ear. "It's just a model, after all."

"I know," I slowly replied, rising to my feet. "But we put so much work into its creation…"

"And you can do so again," the Kelian explained, "But for now, you should finish showing me around."

Bidding farewell to Alyssa, the two of us left the room to resume the tour. As we walked, however, I found myself thinking about Alyssa. I'd always thought she seemed more like a Terran than a Zandu; now, there was someone else who shared my belief.

I needed to investigate this further, and I knew how to do it.

Investigation

After finishing Karia's tour nearly two hours later, I decided to visit Tykvas Shak'zar. I didn't dare ask Alyssa about her past, but her older brother might be persuaded to talk.

Knocking on the hard metal door of Tykvas's room, I heard a faint voice yell, "One second, I'll be right there!"

A moment later, the door was opened, and I found the tall Zandu standing before me. "What do you want?" he asked, clearly curious why I was there.

"Something's come up with your sister," I replied, "But before I can help, I'm going to need some basic information about her past."

"What do you need?"

"When was Alyssa born?" I asked. The Zandu's answer to this question would tell me a lot—if he knew when the girl was born, then I'd know she was a Zandu like him. On the other hand, if he had no idea what Alyssa's birthday was, it'd mean that my suspicions about her origin might be correct after all.

A couple of seconds passed as Tykvas considered my question, then he replied, "I can't remember for sure, but I believe she was born around fifteen years ago. I was only two years old at the time, so I have no recollection of the event, but I know she's my sister."

Slightly disappointed to learn that my theories on Alyssa's true origins were all wrong, I nodded and was about to turn away when Tykvas added, "Now that you bring it up, though, I remember that there was always something strange about Alyssa's birth."

"Yes?" I asked, my interest piqued.

"I don't remember my mother being pregnant with my sister, and even though we have several pictures of my family during that time, none of them give any indication that my mother was pregnant. In fact," the Zandu added after a moment, "She remained quite thin throughout the entire time."

"I see," I softly replied, my mind racing. If Tykvas was correct, something strange was going on here. "Well, I have to go now," I told the Zandu, "But thanks for the help!"

Walking away down the hall, I tried to decide what to do next. Although my theory was becoming more and more likely by the minute, I still needed solid proof, and there was only one place I'd be able to find something like that—the Academy Archives. The Archives of the Galactic Academy contained information on every major event in the past thousand years, so hopefully, I'd be able to find something.

Setting the date modifier to the most likely year of Alyssa's birth, I began searching the archives for any file containing references to both the Zandu and Terrans. Only one document appeared, and I opened it for inspection.

On a midsummer's day nearly fifteen years ago, I quietly read, a Zandu Battlecruiser appeared in the skies over the planet Earth. The Terrans mustered their forces, but then, the strangest thing happened—the Zandu asked for peace. The people of Earth had won their favor, so instead of destroying the Terrans, the leader of the aliens—a young Warlord named Garamak Shak'zar— gave the humans the gift of technology.

Before long, the Terrans' technological output had skyrocketed, and the humans asked what they could do for the Zandu in return for the prosperity they'd received. To the surprise of everyone, Garamak didn't ask for weapons, or soldiers, or even money. He only asked for a single human child that he would raise as his own.

Upon reading this last line, my jaw dropped. I'd read and listened to this story dozens of times back on Earth, but I'd never heard this part before. Fascinated, I read on:

At first, the citizens of the Earth were hesitant to comply with the alien's request. The idea of giving a human child to a being from another world was repulsive to them, and they were about to refuse the Zandu's request when the young President of the United States spoke up.

"After all the Zandu have done for us," he'd declared,

"You're just going to ignore their request? I don't know how the rest of you were raised, but when I was a child, I learned not to break a deal. I have a newborn daughter, whom I love more than life itself—yet, for the good of the Earth, I will give her up."

The transfer ceremony took place later that same day, and so it was that Alyssa Wilson, President's daughter became Alyssa Shak'zar, daughter of the greatest Warlord the Zandu have ever known.

Stunned by this sudden revelation, I dropped my data-pad to the table, where it landed with a soft clunk. There, right before me, was all the evidence I'd been looking for ever since I arrived at the school months earlier.

Now that I had this information, however, I had no idea what the next step should be. If I just told the girl that everything she knew about herself was a lie, she'd be more likely to hate me than hug me.

It would be a delicate operation full of potential danger, but it had to be done. Nodding firmly, I left the archives, never realizing that everything was about to fall apart.

The Announcement

It happened during breakfast on the following day. As usual, I was sitting with my friends, but around the middle of the meal, a familiar voice suddenly called out, "Hello, Jayden. Do you mind if I sit here?"

Looking up to see Karia's shining face, I nodded and replied, "Please, feel free to sit wherever you like."

Thanking me, the young Kelian sat down, just as another voice broke in. "So, Terran, who's your girlfriend?" The question came from Kaiold, my Paranoy...friend, and when I turned to face him, I saw that his face was split by a broad grin.

"This is Karia," I replied, introducing her to the rest of the table. "And while she may be a female friend of mine, there is no romantic aspect to our relationship."

"If you say so," the Paranoy nodded sagely, "But I saw your face when she showed up. Trust me, Jayden, you're in love."

"I...am...not...in...love," I declared, my face flush with...annoyance. "Besides," I added, "What would you even know of love?"

"Well, I love the Cafeteria's Bangori Bean Dip," Kaiold mused, "And I love the most recent Space Raider game, and..."

"That's different," I broke in, shaking my head. "Those are just things you enjoy—you don't love them romantically."

The Paranoy looked like he was about to give me some lamebrain response, but before he could, the PA system suddenly turned on, and Principal Elise's voice declared, "Hello, students of the Galactic Academy. We have a special announcement to make!"

A hush fell over the room as Karia's mother continued, "Yesterday, it was revealed to us that one of our students has been lying about their planet of origin. This is a very serious crime since it could allow the student to take advantage of programs and benefits that are intended for students of other races."

Suddenly, I got a terrible feeling in the pit of my stomach. Were they talking about Alyssa? "We want to investigate this matter further," the Principal added, "So, for now, we are going to keep the identity of the student a secret. You can rest assured, however, that once the truth is discovered, we shall announce the criminal's name publically."

As the PA system shut off, a murmur of excitement swept through the room. Everyone seemed to have a different idea of whom the imposter was, but only I knew the truth. Glancing around the room, I searched for Alyssa, but to my surprise, she was nowhere to be found.

"So, Jayden," Kaiold asked. "Whom do you think the imposter is?"

"I'm sorry," I replied, rising from the table, "But I have to go." Turning, I tried to run off, but a soft hand gripped my arm.

"Where are you going?" Karia asked softly.

"It's...it's just something I have to do," I replied, trying to dodge her question. "Don't worry about it." Shaking my hand free, I walked away, my mind deep in thought. Alyssa didn't always eat at my table—she was a popular girl, after all, and had many friends—but for her to be completely absent from the cafeteria was surprising. Something was going on here, and I needed to find out what.

Exiting the room, I walked down the nearest hall, trying to figure out where Alyssa might have gone. I doubted that she'd gone to class this early, and the vid-gaming room was closed until the end of the school day, so she was most likely either in the study hall or the gymnasium.

The study hall seemed like the more likely option, so I set off in that direction. Arriving a few minutes later, I discovered that my suspicions were correct, and I found Alyssa sitting in a far corner of the room. Instead of studying, however, I discovered that she was crying.

Quietly walking over, I laid a comforting hand on her

shoulder. "What's going on, Alyssa?" I softly asked my voice nothing more than a whisper. "Why are you crying?"

"I just learned that everything I've ever believed was wrong," the girl moaned, "But instead of comfort, I received condemnation." Gently sliding into the seat next to her, I listened as Alyssa continued, "I'm a Terran! All my life, I've thought I was a Zandu, and now…"

"But didn't you ever think you were somehow different?" I asked. "After all, you don't look anything like the other Zandu. They all have purple skin and spiky black hair, while you have normal, human-colored skin and brown hair."

"My 'parents' told me I was an albino," Alyssa replied, the memory bringing a tear to her eye. "It never made sense to me—after all, if I were an albino, I wouldn't have blue eyes, and my hair would be white. Now, I realize they were lying."

Wrapping an arm around her shoulders, I hugged her close. "Don't worry, Alyssa," I told the sobbing girl. "I'll make sure all this gets sorted out."

"Don't believe him," a new voice broke in. "After all, he's the one who revealed your true identity."

Mind Games

Turning in shock, I saw Karia enter the study hall, a strange look on her face. "Yesterday afternoon, Jayden paid a visit to your older brother and asked for information regarding your birth. At the time, Tykvas thought nothing of this request, and he freely told the Terran things that indicated your origins as a non-Zandu."

Pausing for a moment to check the reactions of her audience, the Kelian continued, "After his conversation with Tykvas, Jayden then went to the Academy Archives, where he searched for any records of where you might have come from. To his surprise, he quickly found clear proof that you were a Terran, and he immediately told the Principal all about it."

"What?" I finally broke in, unable to stay quiet any longer. "I didn't do anything of the sort! Sure, I looked up Alyssa's past..."

"Wait," the Zandu girl interrupted, her eyes wide. "You knew I was a Terran, and you didn't tell me?"

"I was waiting for the right moment..."

"The 'right moment' would have been right away!" Alyssa exclaimed. "If I found out a deep, dark secret from your past, would you want me to keep it to myself?"

"Well, technically, he didn't keep it to himself," Karia interjected. "After all, he told my Mother everything."

"No, I didn't," I corrected, "And you're not helping." Pausing for a second to gather my thoughts, I turned to Alyssa and said, "Listen, I'm sorry for not telling you earlier. I didn't want to hurt you…"

"But you did," the Zandu replied. "If you'd just told me, I could have been prepared for all this. Instead, you just talked to the Principal instead, and now I'm going to be expelled!"

I sat up in shock, stunned by Alyssa's announcement. The Principal had mentioned that the 'criminal' would be punished, but she never said that the punishment would be expulsion. "Alyssa," I began.

"No," she exclaimed. "I don't want to hear any more excuses!" Rising from her seat, Alyssa continued, "You are no longer my friend, and if you know what's best for you, you'll never talk to me again." Turning, the Zandu stalked out of the room; her eyes narrowed in anger.

"Well," Karia said as we watched Alyssa go, "That could have gone better."

"This is all your fault," I declared, thrusting a finger in the Kelian's direction. "I may have been the one who found the truth about Alyssa, but I didn't tell anyone about it. You, however, seem to know all about the situation, and your mother is the one handling this investigation."

"What are you saying?" Karia asked hesitantly.

"I'm saying you're the one who revealed Alyssa's secret, not me!" I declared. "And in doing so, you caused the expulsion of the Academy's most popular student." Pausing for a moment, I continued, "Why did you do all this? What do you have to gain?"

"Quite a lot, actually," Karia replied with a little smile. "And it all has to do with you."

"Me?"

Karia laughed as she elaborated, "You see, you're different from the other students at this school. Many of them are handsome, or dashing, or athletic, but—as you just showed by figuring out my little plan—you may be the smartest one of them all. I come from Kelia, where building your mind comes before anything else, so naturally, I find this trait attractive."

"Wait," I slowly interrupted. "Are you saying you're in love with me?"

"Love is a strong word," the Kelian replied thoughtfully. "It's more of an intense fascination/attraction."

"But if that's so, why did you...oh." As I said this, I suddenly realized what Karia was getting at. "No," I declared, "You're completely off the mark."

"Am I?" she asked, "I don't think so. After all, I was there in the machine shop with you and Alyssa. I saw the way you two looked at each other—you were definitely in love."

At this point, everything fell into place. "So that's why you are trying to get Alyssa expelled!" I exclaimed. "You want to have me to yourself. Well," I added after a moment, "It's not going to happen. I'm going to leave right now, and tell everyone what you…"

"Actually," Karia replied, raising a hand, "No, you won't."

I was about to reply to the contrary, but then a tingling sensation ran through my brain. Throwing up my hands, I grabbed my head, trying to stave off the bizarre pain. "You're going to forget everything I just told you," Karia declared, continuing to hold up her hand, "And from now on, you are going to be hopelessly in love with me."

The pain receded a couple of seconds later, and I rose to my feet a changed man. My every thought centered on Karia, the love of my life, and I felt fulfilled. Sure, I'd strangely lost all memory of the past five minutes or so, but that didn't matter. After all, they couldn't have been that important anyway, right?

Cognitive Recalibration

Two hours after the strange encounter with Alyssa and Karia, I floated into the school cafeteria, my face aglow. For perhaps the first time in my life, I was in love with someone, and I knew she loved me back.

Grabbing my lunch, I looked around the room, trying to decide where to sit. Ever since I arrived at the Galactic Academy several months earlier, I'd been sitting with my friends, so I decided that it was time for a change of pace.

Walking over to the back of the room, I sat down at an empty table. Less than a minute later, Karia arrived and took the seat beside me; her delicate mouth spread in a wide smile. "Hello, Karia," I said in greeting, delighted that she'd come over.

"Hello, Jayden," she replied, scooping up a forkful of food. "How are you doing?"

"Now that you're here," I told her with a wink, "Everything's perfect."

Smiling, we returned to eating, but a couple of seconds later, a dark shadow fell over the table before us. "Hello, Jayden," a terrible voice declared, "What are you doing here?"

"It's none of your business, Kaiold," I stated, my voice cold. The Paranoy had been one of my old friends, but that life was done now.

"So you're not sitting over here because Alyssa's at our table?" my former friend asked. "That would make sense because she tells me that you're trying to get her expelled."

Something about Kaiold's statement nagged at my consciousness, but I decided to ignore it as I replied, "I'm not trying to get her expelled—I just want the truth to be known."

"The truth?" the Paranoy asked. "And what truth is that?"

"Alyssa is a Terran," I told my former friend. "But she's been pretending to be a Zandu…" I paused for a moment before continuing, "…so…she can take advantage of special…benefits for that species."

"Really?" Kaiold looked skeptical. "The Alyssa I know would never do something like that."

"Well, apparently you…didn't Know her that well," I replied. I was having trouble speaking as if something in my mind was attempting to stop my words. "She's just a big liar, after all."

"I don't know what's going on, Jayden," the Paranoy shook his head, a disappointed look on his face, "But I don't like it one bit, and until you come to your senses, our friendship is over."

"Don't worry about him," Karia whispered as Kaiold stalked away. "He wasn't a true friend anyway."

"I know," I replied slowly. "I just..." Once again, I could sense a strange conflict in my mind, which made no sense...

"Anyway," Karia broke in, interrupting my train of thought, "I have to go take care of something, but I'll see you later. Bye!" Giving me a quick hug, the Kelian walked away, leaving me alone at the table.

Smiling as a result of the short embrace, I returned to my food. I'd only taken a bite or two, however, when a voice suddenly said, "Jayden Armstrong, I'm disappointed."

Turning, I saw a tall, dark-furred alien sitting in the chair beside me. "Nazo," I growled, my voice harsh. I didn't know why, but something about the mysterious Schaddo set me on edge.

"I had such high hopes for you, and you've let me down," Nazo said, shaking his head sadly.

"What are you talking about?" I asked.

"You defeated a Changeling, rescued Alyssa, exposed a hacker," the Schaddo continued, counting each event off on his finger, "And yet, you let a little girl invade your mind and play with your thoughts."

"What…?" I asked, befuddled. "You…you're lying!"

"The Kelians are a race of psionics!" Nazo exclaimed. "They rip apart men's minds for fun, and that's the least of their abilities. They're also telekinetic, telepathic and…"

"Be quiet!" I broke in, my mind ripping itself apart. Half my brain wanted to believe the Schaddo, while the other half wanted to strangle him to death. "I need to think!"

"No," Nazo replied, "You need to stop thinking." I opened my mouth to object, but then a powerful fist crashed into the side of my head, and the world went black.

***

"Jayden, wake up!"

Jarred back into consciousness by the sudden sound of Nazo's voice, I bolted upright, my eyes wide. "Where…where am I?" I asked, looking around in desperate fear.

"Calm down, Terran," the Schaddo broke in, grabbing my wrists with his powerful hands, "We're still in the cafeteria. Now," he continued, releasing my arms, "How do you feel?"

"Well," I told him, "My head aches and my body feels

sluggish, but my mind seems…clearer, somehow."

"Good," the alien nodded. "That means it worked."

"What worked?" I asked, confused.

"My cognitive recalibration," Nazo replied, his mouth set in a slight smirk. "I knocked you unconscious, which caused your brain to reset. When it did, all traces of Karia's influence were wiped away."

"So does that mean I'm clear?"

"For now," the Schaddo confirmed. "Though from now on, you should steer clear of Karia so she can't brainwash you again."

As he said this, a terrible thought suddenly crossed my mind. "My friends!" I exclaimed. "I need to talk to them!"

"That you do," Nazo agreed. "But first, you might want to go apologies to Alyssa."
Nodding, I asked, "Where is she?"

"I believe she's heading for the hanger," the Schaddo replied, pausing for a moment to think.

"Why would Alyssa be going to the hanger?"

"Because she's about to leave the school."

Apologies and Good-byes

Rushing through the halls, I arrived in the hanger minutes later to find Alyssa entering a small Zandu shuttle. Realizing that there wasn't a moment to lose, I called out, "Alyssa! Don't go!"

At the sound of my voice, the Zandu girl turned, her hatred of me visible on her face. "What is it, Jayden," she asked, her voice dark and angry. "Do you have some other dark secret about me that you want to expose for everyone to hear?"

"No," I broke in. "That's not right at all!"

"Then what are you doing here?"

"I want...I want to apologize," I told her, my face contrite. "I should never have gone digging into your past without your permission. You have a right to your privacy, just like anyone else, and what I did violate that right."

As she listened, Alyssa's expression slowly began to soften, but then she remembered why she was in the hanger in the first place. "Well," she declared, her anger surfacing once more, "That's all great, but it's no excuse for what you did with the information. I'm being expelled—"

"Because of Karia!" I broke in.

"Karia?" Alyssa asked, confused.

"Karia is a Kelian," I explained, "So she has incredible mental powers, including telepathy, which is the ability to read minds. Karia stole the information from my brain and gave it to her mother, who happens to be the principal of the Academy."

"But...why?" the Zandu girl exclaimed. "What have I ever done to her?"
"According to her," I replied, speaking from the memory I'd just recently regained access to, "You were her rival."

"Her rival?" Alyssa asked. "For what?"

The answer to this question was quite embarrassing, to be honest, but if Alyssa were ever to forgive me, I'd need to give her full disclosure. "She thought that you were a rival for my affections."

At this statement, the Zandu's mouth dropped in shock, while simultaneously her cheeks lit up with a deep pink blush. "I...I...I'm not..."

"I'm not saying you are," I told her, though her display was quickly convincing me to the contrary. "But Karia thought you were, so she tried to put a stop to it. Remember when our Zandu Battlecruiser model fell off its stand, despite being bolted down?" Alyssa nodded, and I continued, "I think Karia used her telekinesis to knock it over, in the hopes of making me angry at you.

When that didn't work, she decided to try something else."

"Planting a seed of suspicion in my mind, the Kelian manipulated me into investigating your past," I continued, delighted to see my friend's face softening with every word. "Once I had enough evidence, the Kelian went straight to her mother, demanding your expulsion from the school."

"So it wasn't you after all," Alyssa exclaimed happily. "It was all Karia!"

"That's only partially true," I replied. "Karia's influence was strong, but I could have resisted it if I'd tried. Instead, I was curious, and that curiosity cost you everything." Pausing a moment, I added, "I'm sorry, and if you never want to speak to me again, I'll understand."

Giving me a sorrowful look, Alyssa said, "Jayden, what you did was wrong, and there is no excuse for your actions. Never speaking to you again would be nothing compared to the punishment you deserve." Nodding sadly, I turned to go, but the Zandu girl wasn't done yet. "I'm a big believer in second chances, however, and your apology has given me the hope that you won't mess yours up."

"So that means…?" I asked hopefully.

"We can be friends again," Alyssa replied, smiling broadly.

Overcome with emotion, I just stood there, my eyes wet with...perspiration. "Oh, Jayden," Alyssa laughed, "I'm so glad you got here before I left. I'd have hated to leave with our friendship still in tatters."

I opened my mouth to agree, but before I could, a loud voice declared, "Well, this is all so touching. Too bad it's all about to come to an end."

With a terrible screeching sound, a metal beam detached from the ceiling and plummeted right toward Alyssa. Reacting instantly, I leaped forward and tackled the Zandu, knocking her away seconds before the giant chunk of titanium crashed into the hangar floor.

"What in the galaxy?" Alyssa exclaimed, leaping to her feet.
"Karia," I replied darkly. "She wants to kill you."

Power Overwhelming

"She wants to kill me?" Alyssa exclaimed, stunned by my announcement. "Why would she do that?"

"Why do you think?" I asked. "She wants to eliminate the competition."

"How astute, Jayden!" the Kelian's voice declared, echoing through the hanger. "Now, please get out of the way and let me end this girl's miserable life!"
"I don't think so!" I yelled.

"In that case," Karia replied, "I'll just have to make you do it." I suddenly felt a terrible buzzing sensation at the base of my skull, and clenching my head between both hands I let out a cry of pain.

"Get...out...of...my...head!" I exclaimed, collapsing to my knees. The pain was starting to envelop my entire brain, and I feared that before long my entire mind would break under strain.

At that moment, however, a pair of hands shoved a bulky metal helmet into my arms, and a voice called out, "Jayden, put this on!" Complying with the newcomer's instructions, I lifted the object up and stuffed it over my head. Instantly, the pain went away, and my mind was clear once more.

Rising to my feet, I found Nazo standing beside me, a

narrow smile on his face. "Good work at resisting her," he congratulated me. "There's no time to waste. However—we need to stop her before she destroys the school."

"How has she gotten this powerful?" Alyssa asked. "Can all Kelians do this?"

"In their teenage years, Kelians—especially the females—tend to be emotionally unstable, and lose control of their abilities remarkably easily," Nazo explained. "When they get older, they can usually keep these things under wraps, but the potential danger teenage Kelians pose is the reason why no Kelian has ever been admitted to the Academy."

"Karia was admitted to the Academy under the assumption that her mother would be able to keep her under control. Apparently," Nazo concluded, "That isn't the case."

"So," Alyssa asked nervously, "What's the plan?"

"We need something to protect us from Karia's mental abilities," I replied. "Nazo, do you have any more of these helmets?"

"I don't," the Schaddo replied, "But I know where we can find some. Come on!"

***

As it turned out, every storage locker was equipped with mind-protection helmets like the one I was wearing, along with entire suits to go with them. "In case you were wondering," Nazo told us as we suited up, "These suits are designed for handling hazardous materials. However, the elements used in their construction are also impervious to the energy-wavelength the Kelian psionics use. If we're to be truly safe, we should wear the entire suit."

Deciding the Schaddo's advice was sound, Alyssa and I joined Nazo in donning the intimidating outfits. "So," I asked, slipping my arm into a sleeve, "What's next?"

"Now, we need to find Karia," Nazo replied. "Unfortunately, I don't know where she is, so we might need to search the whole station…"

"Wait for a second," I broke in, holding up a hand. "Can Kelians use their abilities without line of sight?"

"Not really," the Schaddo shook his head. "Unless they have some substitute…"

"Like a surveillance camera?"

Realizing what I was getting at, Nazo nodded, "Yes, that would work."

"In that case," I exclaimed, "I know where she is!"

"Where?" Alyssa asked.

"The Security Control Room!"

***

Our trip to the Security Control Room took nearly fifteen minutes, and during that time Karia launched five separate attacks on our little group. Thanks to Nazo's keen eyes and lightning reflexes, we managed to dodge each one, but by the time we arrived at our destination we were visibly rattled.

"So," Alyssa asked, casting a nervous glance at the imposing titanium door, "What's the plan?"

"Well," I said, thinking deeply, "We could try something sneaky, but since Karia is using the Academy's Security Cameras to watch our every move, sneaking won't accomplish anything."

"So what are you saying?" Alyssa asked. "That we should just walk in and hope for the best?"

"Basically," I replied, understanding her concern. "Look, I know it's not ideal, but right now, it's our best shot."

"Jayden's right," Nazo broke in, nodding his agreement. "Trying to get in any other way would likely be even more dangerous."

"Well, when you put it like that..." Alyssa said, "I guess

I'm in."

"Great!" I exclaimed, throwing open the door. "Let's do this thing!" Charging into the well-lit security room, we found our target sitting at a bank of surveillance monitors; her back turned to us.

"Karia!" I declared, "Your reign of terror is done! Surrender now, and we won't hurt you."

"Oh, you won't hurt me," the Kelian replied, turning to face us. "On the contrary: I'm going to be the one hurting you."

Psionic Showdown

Rising from her seat, Karia cocked her hands back, as if she were about to throw a fastball in our direction. Recognizing this strange act, Nazo cried out, "Get down!" Obeying the Schaddo's orders immediately, we dove to the floor seconds before a ball of purple energy slammed into the wall above us.

"Oh, great," Alyssa exclaimed. "Now she can throw energy!" Nodding my agreement, I leaped to my feet, realizing this fight had just grown much harder.

"Spread out!" Nazo yelled, rushing across the floor. "Get behind her and take her down!"

"Oh, really?" the Kelian asked with a terrible smirk. "Well, if that's your plan, I'll do this!" Raising both hands, Karia laughed as a diaphanous purple substance oozed out of her palms and encircled her in an impenetrable bubble.

"What in the galaxy?" Alyssa asked.

"It's a psion-shield!" Nazo replied, "It's completely impenetrable! On the plus side, though," he added after a second, "While she's in there, she can't attack us."
Just as the Schaddo finished speaking, the entire room suddenly shook, as if the entire station was tearing itself apart from within. "Um, Nazo," Alyssa broke in, "That sure sounds like an attack to me!"

Turning to our opponent, I called out, "Karia, what are you doing?"

"If I can't have you, Jayden," the Kelian replied with a harsh laugh, "Then I'll make sure that no one ever will! I'm going to destroy this station, with all of you in it!"

"But you'll die too!" I exclaimed.

"I don't care," she declared. "Without you, I have nothing to live for—I will welcome death!"

Realizing it was hopeless, I dropped my head. We were all going to die here, and there was nothing I could do about it. Just as I had given up all hope, however, something strange happened. Crying out in agony, Karia clutched her forehead with both hands and collapsed to the ground.

"Um, what's going on?" I asked, confused.

"It's Karia's mother!" Nazo exclaimed. "She's using her abilities to stop the destruction!" As he said this, the young Kelian's psion-shield suddenly dropped, leaving her defenseless.

"Get...her...now!" a disembodied voice cried. "I can't...hold her...much...longer!" Rushing forward, we tackled the disabled girl, pinning her to the ground.

"Stop this madness, Karia!" I exclaimed. "It's not too

late!"

At the sound of my voice, the young Kelian's eyes softened. "You...you're right," she whispered, taking a deep breath. "You always are." Concentrating, the young girl was about to undo the damage her rampage had done when the door was flung open and a security team armed with plasma rifles charged in.

"Everyone hands up!" the squad leader exclaimed. Immediately, all four of us flung our arms skyward, and the man continued, "Which one of you is responsible for the attacks on the Academy?"

"That...that would be me," Karia confessed, her head lowered in shame. "Don't worry, I'll—" Without so much as a word of warning, the leader of the security squad pulled the trigger of his weapon, firing a bolt of superheated plasma at the unarmed Kelian.

Shocked by this sudden action, Karia was unable to do anything but watch as the plasma shot toward her chest. Less than a second before contact, however, a dark object intercepted the boiling projectile and knocked it away into a nearby wall.
"I'm going to give you one warning," Nazo exclaimed, ignoring the astonished stares he was receiving for what he'd just done. "Shoot at an unarmed girl again, and I'll knock the plasma bolt back at you."

"Okay, okay!" the errant guard exclaimed, dropping his weapon. "It won't happen again!" There was a tense pause, then he added, "So, can we take her now?"

"I don't think so," the Schaddo replied. "Right now, I wouldn't entrust you with a single Final, much less a girl's life. I'll take her down personally."

"And if she acts up again?"

"I can handle her," Nazo declared. "But somehow, I don't think that will be an issue."

The End

As Nazo had predicted, Karia followed him without a fight, and before long she had been placed in a secure cell in the Academy Brig. Before we left, the girl apologized for the whole thing, promising that if she were ever allowed to attend the Academy again, she'd make up for all the trouble she'd caused.

Leaving the brig, we returned to the main part of the Academy, where we discovered that we were now celebrities. We'd saved the lives of every single student in the station, and all of them wanted to thank us for our heroism.

Nazo especially got a lot of attention, thanks to the general air of mystery he exuded, along with his deflection of the plasma bolt that would have claimed Karia's life. Like everyone else in the Academy, I was curious as to how the Schaddo had moved so quickly, but when I asked about it, Nazo just cryptically replied, "I controlled the situation's chaos."

I was going to ask for clarification, but then Kaiold came over, his face glowing with excitement. "I heard about you are being mind-controlled!" he exclaimed as he approached. "Now I understand why you were so cold to me earlier."

"Yeah, sorry about that," I told him with a sheepish smile. "I wasn't myself."

"I know," the Paranoy replied. "So, how did you get Karia out of your head?"

"Nazo punched me."

"Oh, cognitive recalibration!" Kaiold exclaimed. "Works every time. So," the Paranoy added after a couple of seconds, "What's happening with Alyssa?"

"I talked briefly to the Principal before coming here," I told my friend. "When she realized that Alyssa had been completely unaware of her origin and that she was adopted into a Zandu family, Principal Elise rescinded all punishments."

"Hey, Alyssa," the Paranoy called out, motioning for the girl to come over. "Have you heard the good news? You can stay!"

"I know," Alyssa replied. "I was there when the Principal made the decision." She was trying to sound unmoved by this turn of fortune, but I could tell that she was just as excited as the rest of us.

"So," I asked, "What's the first thing you're going to do, now that you've been reinstated in the Academy?"

"This," the girl replied, and stepping forward she gave me a quick kiss on the cheek. "That's for saving me," she explained, a slightly shy look on her face.

"If that's so," I replied, "Then I'll be sure to save you much more often."

We laughed, and I realized how fortunate I was. I'd been in three life-threatening situations since I arrived at the Academy, but thanks to my friends I'd made it through every one.

At that moment, I had no idea what lay ahead, but I knew that no matter what happened, I would be ready for it because my friends would be by my side.

End

CHARLIE
BOOK

10602793R00069

Printed in Great Britain
by Amazon